OCTOPUS SHOCKTOPUS!

To all those who welcome newcomers,
whether they have eight legs or two. – P.B.

In memory of our little rescue dog Holly
who lives on in the pages of this book. – S.L.

First published 2020 by Nosy Crow Ltd,
The Crow's Nest, 14 Baden Place, Crosby Row, London SE1 1YW
www.nosycrow.com

ISBN 978 1 78800 267 7 (HB)
ISBN 978 1 78800 268 4 (PB)

Nosy Crow and associated logos are trademarks
and/or registered trademarks of Nosy Crow Ltd.

Text © Peter Bently 2020
Illustrations © Steven Lenton 2020

A CIP catalogue record for this book is available from the British Library.

Printed in China
Papers used by Nosy Crow are made from wood grown in sustainable forests.

1 3 5 7 9 8 6 4 2 (HB)
1 3 5 7 9 8 6 4 2 (PB)

OCTOPUS SHOCKTOPUS!

PETER BENTLY & STEVEN LENTON

One day, we found an octopus
had come to live on top of us.

Our neighbour, Mrs Antrobus,
said, "I don't like that octopus!
An octopus just looks all wrong.
An octopus does **not** belong."

She went and called the fire brigade.
They couldn't shift it, so it stayed.

At first it sat there, looking bored.

It dozed a bit and sometimes snored.

But when our friends came round that day,
we asked it, "Would you like to play?"
We started off by playing catch,
and then we had a football match.

Imagine that – all **eight** of us
against a giant octopus!

Later on, we had more fun –
we jumped its eight legs, one by one.

It gave us all a jolly ride.
It also made a **perfect** slide!

And soon it was quite plain to see
how very useful it could be
to have our friend on top of us,
our **special**, giant octopus.

On mornings that were bright and fine,
it made a handy washing line.

It dug the garden, built a shed,
and helped to paint the whole fence red.

My kite got tangled in our tree.
Our octopus just pulled it free.

It rescued Gracie's teddy, too,
the time she flushed it down the loo.
(From that time on, it smelled of poo!)

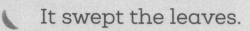It swept the leaves.

It cleared the snow.

It pushed the car to make it go.

And people came from **miles** to see
our **octo-tastic** Christmas tree!

We all **adored** the octopus
who'd come to live on top of us.

And **even** Mrs Antrobus,
grew fonder of our octopus.
Especially when it saved her hat
and rescued Pumpkin Pie, her cat.

Everybody said to us,

"We wish
WE had
an octopus!"

(Except the village baker, Sid,
who said, "I'd rather have a squid.")

One day, we found **no** octopus
was living right on top of us.

Where **had** it gone? We all felt glum.
We missed our massive, eight-legged chum.

But in the night, we heard a bump!
It woke us up and made us jump.

"Yikes!" we said. "What can it be?"
We quickly ran outside to see...

something quite spectacular,
miraculous, tentacular...

...our own
gigantic octopus
was living back on top of us!

But that's not where this story ends...

...our octopus had fetched its friends!